The Three
Little Pigs

Retold and Illustrated by DAVID McPHAIL

Cartwheel ·B·O·O·K·S· ®

Scholastic Inc.

New York   Toronto   London   Auckland   Sydney

For Kiko, Nigel, and Amos:
Three of a kind, all different
—D.M.

Text and illustrations copyright © 1995 by David McPhail.
All rights reserved. Published by Scholastic Inc.
CARTWHEEL BOOKS is a registered trademark of Scholastic Inc.

Library of Congress Cataloging-in-Publication Data
McPhail, David M.
 The Three Little Pigs / written and illustrated by David McPhail.
      p. cm.
 Summary: In this retelling of the traditional tale a little pig saves her brothers and herself from a
wolf's attacks by using her head and planning well.
 ISBN 0-590-48118-5
 [1. Folklore. 2.Pigs—Folklore.] I. Title.
PZ8. 1.M467Th 1995
398.2'4529734—dc20
[E]
                                                                              93-43991
                                                                                  CIP
                                                                                   AC

12 11 10 9 8 7 6 5 4 3 2 1   5 6 7 8 9/9 0/0

Printed in Singapore

First Scholastic printing, March 1995

Once there were three little pigs who lived at home with their mother. When the little pigs were all grown up, they decided to strike out on their own.

One morning at sunrise, they said good-bye to their mother and walked away, arm in arm.

When they came to a crossroads, the three
little pigs took different paths, promising to
visit each other very soon.

The first little pig saw a man cutting straw in a field. The little pig offered to help if the man would give him straw to build his house. And the man agreed.

The little pig carried the straw to a shady
riverbank where he quickly built a little straw
house and settled in.

The second little pig came upon a woman collecting sticks along the edge of a deep, dark forest. The little pig offered to help the woman if she would give him sticks to build his house.

The woman agreed, and by-and-by, she gave
the second little pig some bundles of sticks. The
little pig quickly threw the sticks together in the
shape of a house, crawled in, and went to sleep.

The third little pig met a man who was building a tall chimney out of bricks. But the man was afraid to climb the ladder.

"If you will give me enough bricks to build a small house, I will climb the ladder for you," said the third little pig. And the man agreed.

The man gave the third little pig stacks and stacks of bricks that the little pig took to the top of the highest hill. *This a good place for my house,* thought the third little pig. And she began to build.

The next morning, the first little pig was awakened by a noise outside his house.

He peeked out between pieces of straw, and when he saw the wolf, the little pig trembled, for he knew that wolves were no friends of pigs.

"Little pig, little pig, let me come in," said the wolf.

"Not by the hair of my chinny chin chin," answered the first little pig.

"Then I'll huff, and I'll puff, and I'll blow your house in!" roared the wolf.

So he huffed and he puffed. And while the wolf was blowing the house down, the first little pig ran away and dove into the stream.

When it was safe, the first little pig cautiously made his way to his brother's house of sticks and told his brother how the wolf blew his house down.

At that instant, they heard a noise.
"It's the wolf!" whispered the first little pig.
"There's nobody home," called the second
little pig. "Go away!"

But the wolf didn't budge. "Little pig, little pig, let me come in!" he snarled.

"Not by the hair of my chinny chin chin," replied the second little pig.

"Then I'll huff, and I'll puff, and I'll blow your house in!" roared the wolf.

So he huffed, and he puffed, and as with the straw
house, he blew the stick house right down to the ground.
The two little pigs ran in opposite directions, which so
confused the wolf that, by the time he
decided which one to chase, they
had both disappeared into the
woods.

Later that day, the first little pig and the second little pig arrived at the house of the third little pig. The third little pig welcomed her brothers into her sturdy brick house.

While they told her the story of the wolf,
she lit a fire in the fireplace and set a big kettle
of water on to boil.

Then the three little pigs started to cut some vegetables to make a stew. Suddenly there was a pounding at the door. It was the wolf! The first little pig and the second little pig were terrified.

But the third little pig felt safe in her house of bricks. "Go away, Wolf," she said. "Don't bother us!"

By this time, the wolf was very hungry and very angry that the other little pigs had gotten away from him.

"Little pig, little pig, let me come in!" he roared at the top of his voice.

"Not by the hair of my chinny chin chin," answered the third little pig calmly.

"Then I'll huff, and I'll puff, and I'll blow your house in!" said the wolf.

But no matter how hard he huffed—and no matter how hard he puffed—he couldn't blow the house down. The brick house was too strong. The exhausted wolf sat on the front step to rest.

When he had recovered somewhat from
all that huffing and puffing, the wolf walked
around the little brick house, looking for
another way in.

The windows were too small for him to squeeze through, but when the wolf looked up, he saw a big chimney sticking out of the roof. It was big enough for a big wolf like himself.

The three little pigs could hear footsteps above them. "Run!" cried the first little pig. "The wolf's coming down the chimney!"

"Hide!" squealed the second little pig. "If he catches us, he'll eat us all!"

But the third little pig was not afraid.

"Finish cutting those vegetables," she said, "while I put some more wood on the fire."

The water in the kettle was boiling
furiously when the clever wolf came
sliding down the chimney—SPLASH!—
right into the big pot.

The third little pig slammed the lid on.
And that was the end of the wicked wolf.